MW00368708

This book belongs to:

_____

"To my brilliant son, Jacob.
And to my niece and nephew, Kennedi and
Karter. You are my sunshine and my joy.
Keep your imaginations flowing! I love you."

By J. Christin Fields

Can you smell my socks?

Illustrated by Natalie Vasilica

"Can you smell my socks?
Kai asked his oldest brother.
"What's wrong with you little
guy? Go ask another."

"Can you smell my socks?"
He asked his sister Drew.

She tossed the socks out her room,
shortly after, Kai flew out too.

"Can you smell my socks?"
Kai moved on to his grandfather.
"Maybe in a little while,
can you hand me
that glass of water?"

"Can you smell my socks?"
Asked he to the cat.
The cat turned her tail
& swatted the socks back.

"Can you smell my socks?"
He asked grandma too.
"A little while later,
when we get back
from the zoo."

"Can you smell my socks?
My favorite Uncle Jay."
"If I smell your socks,
I'm sure my head
will spin for days."

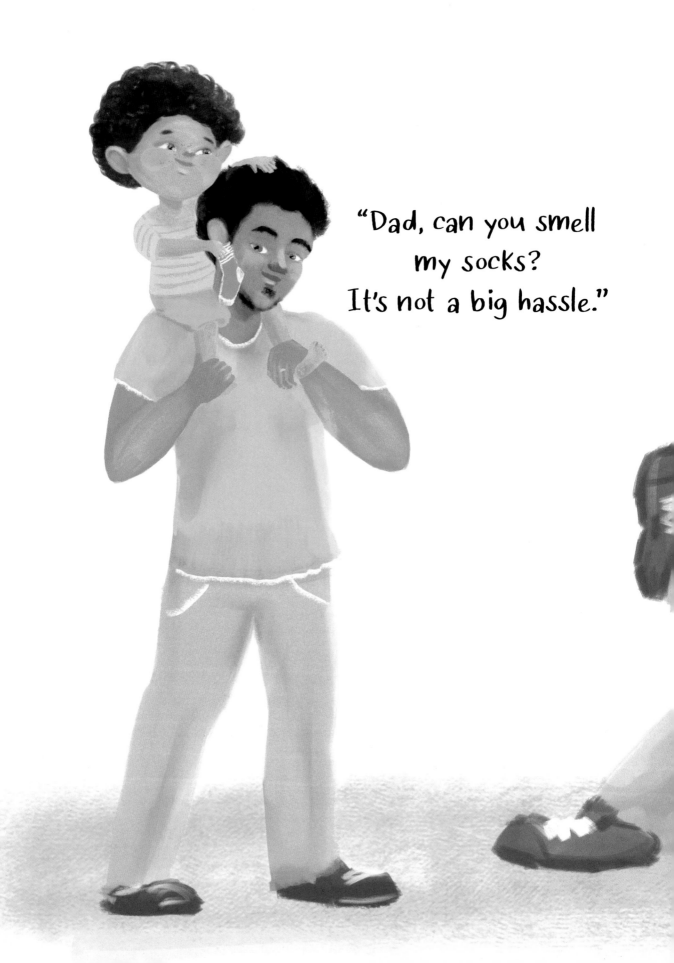

"Dad, can you smell
my socks?
It's not a big hassle."

Instead he picked Kai up &
the two began to wrestle.

"No one will smell my socks," he said.
Not my sister or brother.

"WAIT!," he yelled with hope in heart,
"I'll go ask my mother."

To her parlor he ran, with great haste.
He ran straight to her, hugging her waist.

"Mommy, can you smell my socks?"
She paused & she grinned.
And she smelled his socks,
"Whew!, time to wash these again!"

"But first let me see my tiny boy's feet."
She tickled & kissed them, but the socks she
did keep.

An hour later, here Mommy came.
"Kai, Can you smell these socks?"
"Yes, they are fresh & clean again!"

Made in the USA
Columbia, SC
07 July 2020

13472354R00015